This Walker
book belongs to:

_____

_____

_____

First published 2015 by Walker Books Ltd, 87 Vauxhall Walk, London SE11 5HJ ● 10 9 8 7 6 5 4 3 2 1 ● Text © 2015 Phyllis Root ●
Illustrations © 2015 Helen Craig ● The right of Phyllis Root and Helen Craig to be identified as author and illustrator respectively of this work has
been asserted by them in accordance with the Copyright, Designs and Patents Act 1988 ● This book has been typeset in Calligraphic Antique ●
Printed in Malaysia ● All rights reserved. No part of this book may be reproduced, transmitted or stored in an information
retrieval system in any form or by any means, graphic, electronic or mechanical, including photocopying, taping and
recording, without prior written permission from the publisher. ● British Library Cataloguing in Publication Data: a
catalogue record for this book is available from the British Library ● ISBN 978-1-4063-6230-5 ● www.walker.co.uk

SNOWY SUNDAY

written by
Phyllis Root

illustrated by
Helen Craig

WALKER BOOKS
AND SUBSIDIARIES
LONDON · BOSTON · SYDNEY · AUCKLAND

One Sunday on Bonnie Bumble's farm, snowflakes as big as balls of wool fell. Everyone shivered and shuddered and shook.

"M-m-m-moo,"
mooed the cow.

"Qu-qu-qu-quack,"
quacked the duck.

"Cl-cl-cl-cluck,"
clucked the hens.

"B-b-b-bow w-w-w-wow,"
barked Spot.

"This will never d-d-d-do," chattered Bonnie Bumble. So she got busy with needles and wool.

She knitted boots for Spot.
A scarf for the duck.

A shawl for the sheep.
And a coat for the cow.

Horn-warmers. Beak-warmers. Tail-warmers. Hats all round. Bonnie knitted and knitted and knitted them all.

Still everyone looked shivery and cold.

So Bonnie knitted and knitted
and knitted some more.
The sun came close to
see what was up.

He loved his new hat that Bonnie had made. He beamed and beamed and warmed up the farm. Now everyone was toasty again.

And whenever a snowflake
floated by, Bonnie knitted
it a hat of its own.

For Cindy ~ P.R.   •   To Adèle Geras, an enthusiastic knitter. With love ~ H.C.

Also by Phyllis Root and Helen Craig:

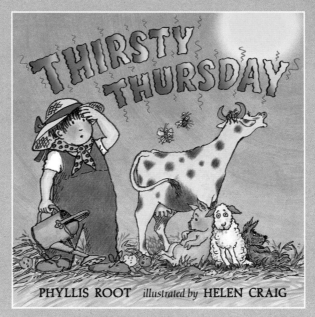

ISBN:978-0-7445-7328-2

Phyllis Root is the award-winning author of many beloved picture books, from the lyrical *Ten Sleepy Sheep* and *Sam Who Went to Sea*, to the rollicking *One Duck Stuck*, *Toot Toot Zoom!*, *Rattletrap Car* and *Big Mama Makes the World*, illustrated by Helen Oxenbury. This is her seventh title in the Bonnie Bumble series. Phyllis lives in Minnesota, in the USA, where snowflakes almost as big as balls of wool frequently fall.

Helen Craig is a widely acclaimed illustrator of books for children, including *This Is the Bear* by Sarah Hayes, *Amy's Three Best Things* by Philippa Pearce, and the hugely popular Angelina Ballerina stories by Katharine Holabird. About this book, she says, "I've loved drawing all seven days of Bonnie's wonderful week – I just wish there were more!" Helen lives in Cambridge.